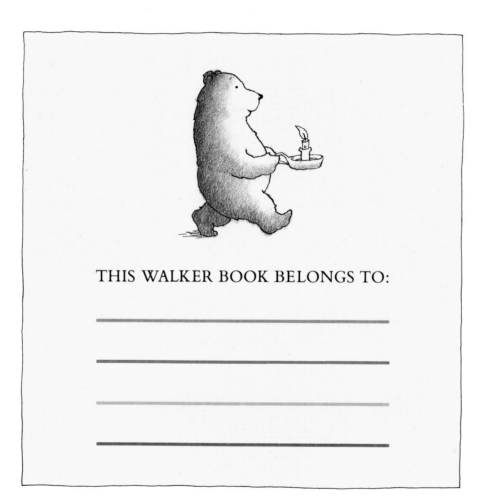

THIS WALKER BOOK BELONGS TO:

First published 1990 by Walker Books Ltd
87 Vauxhall Walk, London SE11 5HJ

This edition published 1992

© 1990 Shirley Hughes

Printed and bound in Hong Kong by
South China Printing Co. (1988) Ltd

British Library Cataloguing in Publication Data
A catalogue record for this book is
available from the British Library.
ISBN 0-7445-2357-5

A Tale of Trotter Street

The Snow Lady

Shirley Hughes

WALKER BOOKS
LONDON

Sam's real name was Samantha but everyone called her Sam.
Sam's dog was named Micawber but everyone called him Mick.
Sam and Mick were very fond of each other.

In the mornings, when Sam went to school and Sam's mum and
dad and her big sister Liz went to work, Mick stayed at home to
guard the house.

When school was over Sam walked home with her friend Barney and his dad. As soon as Mick heard Sam's footsteps he put his front paws on the window-sill and barked a joyful welcome. Sam longed to put him on his lead right away and run off up Trotter Street, with Mick pulling her along and sniffing excitedly at gates and lamp posts. But Mum was still at work and, as usual, she had arranged for Mrs Dean next door to keep an eye on Sam until everyone else came home.

Mrs Dean lived alone with her cat Fluff. Her house was very clean
and tidy. The lace curtains were snowy white and the floor was
polished like a skating rink. Mrs Dean welcomed Sam with a glass
of milk and two plain biscuits. Sam balanced them on her lap and
tried not to drop crumbs while she and Fluff and Mrs Dean sat side
by side on Mrs Dean's beautiful blue sofa and watched television.

Mick was never allowed into Mrs Dean's house. He and Fluff got
on very badly whenever they met. Sam could hear him howling
mournfully next door.

"Whatever has got into that dog?" said Mrs Dean. She opened her front door and shushed at Mick from the doorstep, but he didn't take a bit of notice. He just went on howling.

Sam and Mick were both glad when they heard Mum's key in the lock. Mrs Dean's garden was just as neat and tidy as her house. If Mick got in there and started to dig holes searching for imaginary rabbits, or picked a fight with Fluff, Mrs Dean became very cross.

Mrs Dean didn't even like Mick to be in the street. Sam and Barney and the other children often played in Trotter Street after school and Mick always joined in. But before long Mrs Dean's face would appear at her window. She would tap sharply on the pane, then put out her head and say to Sam:

"That dog really ought to be chained up. My poor little Fluff is so frightened she daren't come out."

Or she would say: "Would you mind asking your friends not to sit on my wall?" Or: "A little less noise, dear, please." And that was the end of their game.

But now the weather was getting too cold to play out of doors. One night the water from a leaking drain froze on the pavement outside Sam's house, turning it into a sheet of ice. The Trotter Street children had a great time running up to it as fast as possible and seeing how far they could slide. They hung on to one another and all slid together in a chain. Wheee! It was just like the Winter Olympics! Mick ran alongside, skidding and barking.

Soon Mrs Dean popped out wearing a shawl over her shoulders. "That's very dangerous," she said. "You might easily break your arms or legs! Do stop at once."

Everyone stopped sliding except Barney. He was at the end of the chain and just kept going. He cannoned into Harvey. Harvey cannoned into Billy, who fell against Mae, who slipped over, pulling Sam and the others with her. There was a terrific pile-up.

"I'm glad Mrs Dean doesn't live next door to us," Barney said later, when he and Sam were drying their feet. "She's always interfering and she hardly ever smiles. She's an old meanie. Mean Mrs Dean, I call her!"

It was getting near to Christmas. People in Trotter Street were buying Christmas trees and putting up decorations. Mrs Dean hung a wreath of plastic holly tied with red ribbons on her door.

Everyone admired it except Mick, who took a savage dislike to it. He barked fiercely every time he caught sight of it. Sam had a terrible time trying to drag him past Mrs Dean's house whenever they went for a walk.

One day Mick got out on
his own and worried the
ribbon until he got one
end of it between
his teeth.

Then he pulled the whole thing down and ran off up Trotter Street
with the wreath round his neck and the ribbons streaming out behind.
Mrs Dean was very cross indeed. After that, Mick was in bad disgrace.

Sam was pleased when she heard Mrs Dean telling Mum that she was planning to spend Christmas with her married son. And sure enough, on the very day before Christmas Eve, Sam saw her setting out in a taxi, taking Fluff in a cat basket and a great many parcels. Hurrah! thought Sam.

Then something even better happened. Out of a slate-grey sky it began to snow. Big flakes whirled down, covering the pavements and parked cars of Trotter Street with a soft, white blanket.

Next morning the sun came out and so did Sam and Barney. They decided to build a snowman where the snow lay thickest, between Sam's front gate and Mrs Dean's. First they piled the snow into a big heap. Mick watched with interest.

Soon there was something which looked like a person with a round head, stick arms and stones for eyes, nose and mouth.

"Let's give him a top hat and a scarf and a pipe," said Barney. "Then he'll be a real snowman!"

Sam and Barney went indoors. Mum was busy but she said they could pick out some old clothes from the top of the cupboard if they liked.

But Sam and Barney could not find any of the things they wanted, only a lot of hats and dresses belonging to Mum and Liz.

"It'll just have to be a snow lady," Sam decided.

They dressed the snow lady in hat and coat, put a shawl over her shoulders and hung a handbag on one of her stick arms. She looked very realistic.

"I know who she reminds me of," said Barney. And he moved the stones so that her mouth turned down instead of up.

He searched in the snow for some more small stones and arranged them where the snow lady's feet would have been. The words stood out clearly:

Sam giggled. The snow lady really did look rather like Mrs Dean. But Barney had not finished. He rearranged the D in Dean to make an M. Then the stones read:

"Lucky she's away," said Sam. "How awful it would be if she could see it!" Then they heard Mum calling and ran indoors taking Mick with them.

The rest of the day was so busy and exciting that Sam and Barney forgot all about the snow lady.

Late that night, long after Barney had wished them all a Happy Christmas and gone home to hang up his stocking, Sam was too excited to sleep. She got up, drew the curtains back a little and looked out at the street. Everything looked white and Christmassy, but big black clouds were scudding across the moon. When she caught sight of the snow lady, still standing there all alone, it gave her quite a shock.

Then Sam saw a taxi draw up. Out stepped Mrs Dean! The driver unloaded Fluff and the luggage and helped her into the house. Mrs Dean walked right past the snow lady without even glancing at her. But she'll see her tomorrow when it's light, thought Sam. It will hurt her feelings. And on Christmas Day too!

Sam decided she must go out at once and kick away the stones which spelled out the snow lady's name. She would take off the clothes too.

It was *terribly important!*

Sam crept quietly downstairs and began to put on her coat over her pyjamas. But Mick heard her and came running into the hall, barking and making a great fuss.

Mum put her head round the living room door. "Whatever are you doing, Sam? You can't possibly go out at this time of night!" And she packed Sam firmly off upstairs. "The sooner you're asleep the sooner Christmas will be here," she said, kissing her good-night.

Still Sam could not get to sleep. She felt too awful about Mrs Dean. When she did fall asleep her dreams were full of excited visions of Mick, Fluff and the snow lady and lots of Christmas parcels all tied up with yards and yards of red ribbon. Mrs Dean was inside one of the parcels. She jumped out and then they were all running and running… But it was not feet which Sam heard in her sleep. It was rain.

When Sam woke up it was still dark. Christmas morning! And yes, the stocking at the foot of her bed was full of exciting surprises. But Sam did not put on her light yet.

Instead she ran to the window. She could hardly see out because rivulets of water were streaming down the pane. Below, in the street, Sam could just see the snow lady. She seemed to have slumped back against the gate post and all around her lay a puddle of water.

Then a great, warm hope leapt up inside Sam. She skipped back into bed and began to open her stocking.

As soon as Christmas Day
had begun properly and all
the family had kissed each
other and given their presents,
Sam slipped out of the front
door.

It had stopped raining.
The snow lady had
collapsed altogether.
Her hat had fallen over
her face and her clothes
were limp and dripping.

She kicked the stones and scattered
them about. Then she picked up
the snow lady's clothes
and pushed them
into the dustbin.

She was only just in time. Mrs Dean's front door opened and out came Mrs Dean, dressed for church.

Mum hurried to their doorstep to call out "Merry Christmas, Mrs Dean! I didn't know you'd come back!"

"A merry Christmas to you all, Mrs Robinson. My son and his wife have 'flu and couldn't have me to stay after all," said Mrs Dean.

"Then of course you must come and have Christmas dinner with us," Mum said at once.

"Why, thank you! That's very kind," said Mrs Dean. And her face melted.

Sam stood right in front of what was left of the snow lady. The name which had stood out so clearly in the snow was now just a jumble of stones lying in a pool of water. Sam shuffled them about with her feet, just in case.

"I expect you wish the snow had lasted longer," Mrs Dean said to Sam.

"Oh no, I don't mind a bit, really," said Sam. And she gave Mrs Dean one of her biggest most Christmassy smiles.

MORE WALKER PAPERBACKS
For You to Enjoy

Some more Tales of Trotter Street

ANGEL MAE

Mae Morgan is chosen to play the angel Gabriel in the school Nativity play. But will the family's new baby steal her glory?

"One of Shirley Hughes' best ever picture books… Ideal for three to seven year olds."

Tony Bradman, Parents

0-7445-2032-0   £3.99

WHEELS

From roller-skates to racing bikes, the wheels are out on Trotter Street! But for Billy and Carlos, on their slow old bikes, racing isn't much fun – and each hopes his birthday will bring a speedy new set of wheels…

"Shirley Hughes' distinctive pictures full of detail and humour depict children just as they are – varied, individual and vibrant."

Junior Education

0-7445-2012-6   £3.99

THE BIG CONCRETE LORRY

For the Pattersons, building an extension is no easy matter, even with the neighbours' help – especially when the concrete is the quick-setting kind!

"A must for any collection… Under fives will enjoy seeing the chaos and confusion unfold."

Tony Bradman, Parents

0-7445-2033-9   £3.99